Breakfast

Around the World

30 Incredible Breakfast Recipes from 30 Diverse Countries

BY: Nancy Silverman

COPYRIGHT NOTICES

My Heartfelt Thanks and A Special Reward for Your Purchase!

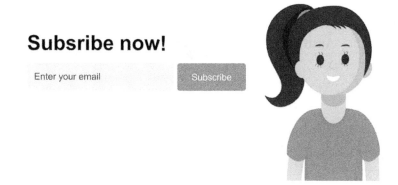

https://nancy.gr8.com

My heartfelt thanks at purchasing my book and I hope you enjoy it! As a special bonus, you will now be eligible to receive books absolutely free on a weekly basis! Get started by entering your email address in the box above to subscribe. A notification will be emailed to you of my free promotions, no purchase necessary! With little effort, you will be eligible for free and discounted books daily. In addition to this amazing gift, a reminder will be sent 1-2 days before the offer expires to remind you not to miss out. Enter now to start enjoying this special offer!

Table of Contents

(1) USA – Blueberry Pancakes with Bacon & Maple Syrup

To me, nothing speaks to my food-devouring soul about the States like gorgeous, fluffy American pancakes. Those babies are good with almost any topping, but nothing could be more all-American than blueberries, crispy bacon and maple syrup (we might borrow that part from Canada, shh!)

Yield: 3

Cooking Time: 35 minutes + 60 minutes resting time

Ingredient List:

- 7 ½ of oz. milk
- 6 slices American-style streaky bacon
- 5 ½ oz. plain flour
- 2 ¾ oz. blueberries + extra for topping
- 1 egg
- 1 Tbsp. baking powder
- 1 Tbsp. caster sugar
- Pinch of salt
- Butter for frying
- Maple syrup for dressing

|||||||||||||||||||||||||||||||||||||||||||||||||||||||||||||

Instructions:

Our recipes allows for 3 pancakes and 2 slices of bacon per person, but don't let us set limits for you! If breakfast is your thing, then go crazy and make as many pancakes as you wish! Wash it all down with some good ol' strong Americano coffee.

1) In one bowl, sieve together the flour, baking powder and sugar with a pinch of salt. In another bowl, beat together the milk and egg.

2) Stir the milk mixture along with the blueberries into the flour mix.

3) Allow the batter to sit for an hour.

4) Pancakes are infinitely superior when served immediately, so we'll prepare the bacon whilst the batter is sitting. Place a frying pan on the heat and before letting it heat up, immediately place the bacon in. You don't need oil, as there is enough fat for it to cook without sticking. Keep the heat on low and allow the bacon to cook, turning it regularly. After 10-15 minutes, it should be almost at the desired level of crispiness. Place on paper towels to drain the excess fat. You can then keep the bacon warm in an oven on low heat.

5) Add a knob of butter into a frying pan and fry the 12 pancakes, using approximately 2 fl oz. of batter for each pancake. The pancake is ready to be flipped when the bottom has become solid, and the bubble in the mixture have all popped.

6) Serve a stack of 3 pancakes with 2 slices of bacon per person. Pop in a few extra blueberries, and cover with a generous drizzle of maple syrup.

Tips: Try not to mix the blueberries so much that they start to breakdown. Keeping them whole will add flavour and moisture to the pancake whilst avoiding creating mush.

Layer on a pretty thick layer of batter into the pan to ensure the thick, fluffy pancakes that the USA is known and loved for.

(2) Australia – Vegemite & Damper

First things first, apologies for being wildly stereotypical here – I know that not all Australians love Vegemite. But I love Australia, and I wanted it to be featured in here. So what could be more quintessentially Australian than Vegemite! Here is a DIY Vegemite recipe – love it or hate it!

Yield: 4-6

Cooking Time: 40 minutes

Ingredient List:

- 8 Tbsp. black tahini
- 4 cups self-rising flour
- 3 Tbsp. soy sauce
- 1 1/3 Tbsp. apple cider vinegar
- 1 cup milk
- 1 Tbsp. butter
- 1 tsp. yeast
- Pinch of salt
- Pinch of pepper

||||||||||||||||||||||||||||||||||||||||||||||||||||||||||||

Instructions:

As with any homemade bread, it's for sure best served warm and fresh! Spread the 'Vegemite' in the fresh damper, careful not to spread too much though, as this is strong stuff! Be extra Aussie and spread some 'avo' on there too.

1) Preheat the oven to 425°F and place some greaseproof paper on a baking tray.

2) Mix the flour with a pinch of salt and then cut in the butter.

3) Make a well in the centre of the flour mixture and then pour in the milk and ½ cup of water. Mix together until everything combines to form a dough.

4) On a floured surface, form the dough into a round loaf, roughly 8 inches in diameter. Then, place the loaf on the baking tray and cut a cross shape on the top of the loaf.

5) Bake for 25 minutes, and then lower the temperature to 350°F and bake for another 5-10 minutes until golden brown.

6) Whilst the loaf is baking, mix the tahini, soy sauce, apple cider vinegar and yeast and season with salt and pepper. Store the homemade Vegemite in the fridge whilst waiting for the loaf to finish.

Tips: If you're looking to be authentic, then damper was traditionally cooked over the dying embers of a campfire – give that a go!

Taste the Vegemite as you're making it. It traditionally is supposed to be very salty, by you may wish to modify to your taste.

(3) Wales - Rarebit

Especially if you're a Brit, you'll know that there is almost nothing in the world more comforting than Mum's cheese on toast. Our American cousins will be familiar with the grilled cheese too. Welsh Rarebit is essentially the greatest cheese on toast or grilled cheese that you will ever eat, with so many more flavors included just to pack that salty and home-y punch.

Yield: 2

Cooking Time: 35 minutes

Ingredient List:

- 8 oz. strong cheddar cheese
- 4 Tbsp. Guinness or another dark beer
- 4 slices granary bread
- 2 tsp. Worcestershire sauce
- 2 tsp. flour
- 1 Tbsp. butter
- 1 tsp. mustard
- Pinch of black pepper
- Parsley to garnish

|||||||||||||||||||||||||||||||||||||||||||||||||||||

Instructions:

In true British fashion, serve with brown sauce and a strong 'cuppa.'

1) Grate the cheese.

2) Add into a saucepan the cheese, along with the Worcestershire sauce, flour, butter, mustard and a shake of pepper. Mix well.

3) Add in the Guinness one Tbsp. at a time, stirring for a minute or so in between each addition. If the mixture looks very wet, leave out the remaining Guinness. Once everything is well melted together, leave to one side.

4) Toast the bread only on one side. This will be easier on the grill or in a pan than in a toaster!

5) Divide the mixture between the 4 slices, spreading it on the untoasted side. Brown it for another minute or 2 under the grill and add on a small amount of fresh parsley to garnish.

Tips: We advise putting in less Guinness as opposed to adding extra flour to avoid floury globs in the mixture and making it taste too floury.

You can variate in this and make it almost like a fondue, serving the rarebit mix in a bowl and cutting the toast into strips to dip.

(4) Bahamas – Grits & Shrimp

For those of us who love a big, savory breakfast, then maybe the Bahamas is the land of our hearts. A traditional breakfast on the island is grits & shrimp. If you're unfamiliar with grits, it was once described to me as "thick and filling. It'll stick to your insides!" Well, if that hasn't convinced you to give this recipe a try then I don't know what will!

Yield: 4

Cooking Time: 60 minutes

Ingredient List:

- 14 oz. peeled shrimp
- 4 tsp. lemon juice
- 3 Tbsp. butter
- 2 Tbsp. parsley
- 2 garlic cloves
- 2 cups cheddar cheese
- 1 ½ cups bacon
- 1 cup unprepared grits
- 1 onion
- Pinch of salt
- Pinch of black pepper

||||||||||||||||||||||||||||||||||||||||||||||||||||||||||

Instructions:

If you are ready for some fire in the belly early in the morning, add some chopped chilli pepper in with the shrimps and start your day off with a bang!

1) Begin heating 4 cups of water in a pan and season with salt and pepper.

2) Once the water is boiling, add in the cup of grits and cook for 20-25 minutes, until the water is absorbed.

3) Once the grits are almost done, grate in the cheese and butter and stir well until everything is melted together. Taste and season more if necessary.

4) In a frying pan, begin by browning off the bacon, which will have been chopped up small. Ensure that there is enough fat in the pan and add in the shrimp to cook, turning them so that they cook evenly and keeping an eye on them as they will quickly overcook.

5) Chop the onion, garlic, and parsley and once the shrimp are pink all over, all them into the pan, along with the lemon juice.

6) Sauté for another 3 minutes and then serve the grits together with the shrimp.

Tips: If possible, multi-task and prepare the shrimp element whilst the grits is cooking down. This means that everything can be fresh and ready at the same time and will avoid things either getting cold or over-cooking.

For mainly aesthetic purposes, larger, whole shrimp are best as they look real good on the plate.

(5) Israel – Shakshukah & Challah Bread

We have been reliably informed that in Israel breakfast means one thing – shakshukah! This is a spicy and flavorsome tomato base topped with egg, and we've included a recipe for traditional Challah bread, which is the only thing to mop up those leftover juices with!

Yield: 6

Cooking Time: 130 minutes

Ingredient List:

- 28 oz. peeled canned tomatoes
- 10 eggs
- 7 garlic cloves
- 4 cups spinach
- 3 ½ cups plain flour
- 2 ½ Tbsp. sugar
- 2 Tbsp. honey
- 2 onions
- 1 ½ tsp. ground black pepper
- 1 Tbsp. olive oil
- 1 Tbsp. sweet paprika
- 1 Tbsp. cumin
- 1 tsp. ground caraway
- 1 jalapeño
- 1 bay leaf
- 1 green pepper
- ¼ oz. active yeast
- ¼ cup tomato paste
- Pinch of salt
- Oil for frying

Instructions:

Make the bread at the same time so that it's warm and fresh when served alongside the spicy Shakshukah.

1) Stir the yeast into 1 cup of warm water, being at a temperature of roughly 100°F. Leave aside for about 10 minutes, until a foamy layer appears on top.

2) Beat 3 eggs and stir them into the yeast with the honey and a pinch of salt.

3) Mix in the flour, a little at a time, until you have a sticky dough. Sprinkle a little extra flour on a surface and in the dough and knead well for 5 minutes.

4) Swirl the olive oil around in a bowl, and place the ball of dough in there, turning a few times to coat the outside in oil. Cover with a damp cloth and leave in a warm area to allow the dough to rise until it's covered in size. This should take 45-60 minutes.

5) Preheat the oven to 350°F.

6) Traditional Challah bread is braided, so here is the technical part! Cut the dough into 3 equal-sized pieces. With your fingertips, roll the 3 pieces into long sausage or rope shaped strings, about 12 inches long. Press the 3 ends together and then braid. If you don't know how, here's an explanation – take the strand farthest to the right and place it over the top of the middle strand. Then do the same with the one farthest to the left, placing it over what has now become the middle strand. Repeat this, taking the farthest left and then right over the middle strand until the end. Then stick the 3 ends together.

7) Line a baking tin with greaseproof paper and place the loaf on top. Separate another egg and use the yolk to egg wash the top and sides of the loaf.

8) Bake for 30-35 minutes until golden brown.

9) Whilst baking, you can prepare the Shakshukah. Heat some oil in a pan to sauté the onion once you've chopped it. Chop the pepper and jalapeño, and add after about 5 minutes.

10) Chop the garlic and then add it to the pan, along with the tomato paste.

11) If the canned tomatoes are whole, crush them slightly before now stirring them into the pan.

12) Add the bay leaf, all of the spices, sugar and a pinch of salt and taste, adding more spices to taste. Allow the mixture to simmer for 20 minutes.

13) Remove the bay leaf and layer on the spinach.

14) On top, crack the remaining 6 eggs, and add the remaining white from the egg separated earlier if you wish. Cover and cook until the whites are no longer translucent, roughly another 10 minutes.

15) By this time, the bread should've been out and cook for 5-10 minutes. Tear in into chunks and serve alongside the Shakshukah.

Tips: In time, you'll find the spice mix that is perfect for you. Experiment with changing the amounts of spice until you find that sweet spot that has your taste buds singing.

Check the bread after 25 minutes, to avoid overcooking. It's way yummier with a soft and doughy centre.

(6) Uzbekistan – Behi

My Uzbek, unfortunately, needs a little work, so we've inky got one word for this title. But it's a word that is close to the heart of many Uzbeks – it means quince. Given that Uzbekistan is the world's third largest grower of quince, it's no surprise that these fruits make up a large part of an Uzbek brek! This recipe is for honey and pistachio baked quince. To me, that sounds like the perfect sweet dish to get my day going on a cold morning!

Yield: 4

Cooking Time: 90 minutes

Ingredient List:

- 8 tsp. honey
- 4 quince
- 1 lemon
- ½ cup pistachios
- ½ cup walnuts
- 1 tsp. cinnamon

||||||||||||||||||||||||||||||||||||||||||||||||||||||||||

Instructions:

In Uzbekistan, nothing comes without traditional Uzbek tea. The most common choices are a green tea or black tea, both taken without milk or sugar. Add a little honey in to sweeten it up if you wish.

1) Preheat the oven to 350°F.

2) Slice up the lemon and place it in a casserole dish along with 1 cup of water.

3) Chop the pistachios and walnuts and stir them in together with the cinnamon.

4) Halve each quince lengthways. Remove the core (if you're not familiar with quince, this looks very similar to an apple core, so you'll easily be able to identify it). Hollow each half a little more to create a cavity to fill. Once done, place them in the lemon and water to prevent browning.

5) Add the scrapings from the quince to the nuts and mix well.

6) Place a tsp.'s worth of honey into the cavity of each quince half and then divide the nut mixture evenly between all 8 halves.

7) Place the quince skin side down into the casserole dish and cover the top with foil. Then, bake for 60-75 minutes, until the quince are tender.

8) Drizzle on another tsp. of honey and serve hot.

Tips: How to pick a quince? Ripe quince are yellow, although slightly on the greener side will still work for this recipe. The stem should have a little white fuzz on it and don't be alarmed by lumps and bumps!

If quince is not readily available in your area, then you should know that they are somewhere between an apple and a pear so that you could switch in either to this recipe for ease.

(7) Belarus - Draniki

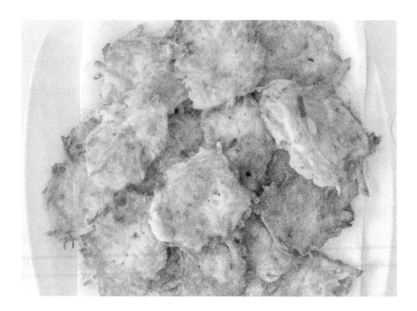

Many cultures have their take in the humble potato pancake, it's true. We have been reliably informed though, that native Belarusian potatoes have fluffy qualities like none other. Obviously, these can be made with any kind of potatoes you have to hand, but if you can find some Belarusian ones, prepare yourself for the fluff!

Yield: 16

Cooking Time: 20 minutes

Ingredient List:

- 12 potatoes
- 4 cloves garlic.
- 1 onion
- 1 cup sour cream
- ½ cup chives or spring onion
- Pinch of salt
- Oil for frying

||||||||||||||||||||||||||||||||||||||||||||||||||||||||

Instructions:

These are best served hot, with a dollop of sour cream and a sprinkling of chives or spring onion.

1) Peel the potatoes and grate them into a bowl.

2) Do the same with the onion and garlic, grating onto and mixing into the potato.

3) Add a pinch of salt and make sure that the mix is well combined.

4) Heat some oil in a large pan, just so hot that it's spitting. Take a large Tbsp.ful of the mixture and pat it into a rough round using your fingers. Fry for 2-3 minutes on each side, until crisped up and golden.

Tips: This is a basic recipe, staying true to the traditional Belarusian dish. If you want to jazz it up though, feel free to add in whatever herbs and spices you desire.

This will work best using a larger grate for the potatoes and a smaller one for the onion and garlic.

(8) Switzerland – Muesli

Try to contain your yodels of delight because here is an incredibly easy, yummy and healthy recipe for that Swiss staple, muesli. Yes, muesli is readily available in the shops, but it often works out much cheaper, and way more satisfying, to make your own. So here it is!

Yield: 8

Cooking Time: 5 minutes

Ingredient List:

- 8 cups oats
- 2 cups raisins
- 2 tsp. cinnamon
- 1 ½ cups flaked almonds
- 1 ½ cups dried apricots
- 1 cup sunflower seeds
- 1 cup chopped date
- 1 cup dried cranberries

‖‖

Instructions:

I'm not going to patronize you by telling you how to pour milk over your muesli. Instead, I suggest using this muesli as a base for some delicious overnight oats recipes or topping a bowl of fruit and yoghurt.

1) Mix all the ingredients, adding a little more of your favorites if you want!

2) Boil 2 cups of water, and then pour the mixed ingredients in.

3) Turn the heat down low and cook until the water has been absorbed. This will take probably 10-15 minutes.

4) Cover the pan for a further 5 minutes and allow it to sit off of the heat before serving.

Tips: Keep mixing whilst on the heat in the pan to avoid sticking and burning!

For thick and creamy overnight oats, use milk or a milk alternative instead of water in this process and then chill.

(9) Bolivia – Salteñas

La Paz in Bolivia is situated up in the mountains, the height of which almost rivals some of the Rockies. This means that whilst it's amazing and beautiful, it can be pretty chilly in a morning! What can warm you up though, both inside and out, is a fresh, warm salteña, which is the yummy Bolivian equivalent to an empanada.

Yield: 25

Cooking Time: 35 minutes

Ingredient List:

- 35 oz. beef loin
- 24 oz. potato
- 8 Tbsp. vegetable oil
- 4 cups liquid beef stock
- 3 ½ oz. lard
- 3 ½ oz. raisins
- 3 cups plain flour
- 3 onions
- 2 Tbsp. turmeric powder
- 2 Tbsp. chili powder
- 2 Tbsp. chopped parsley
- 1 ½ oz. gelatin
- 1 egg
- 1 Tbsp. ground black pepper
- 1 Tbsp. oregano
- ½ cup sugar
- Pinch of salt

IIIIIIIIIIIIIIIIIIIIIIIIIIIIIIIIIIIIIIIIIIIIIIIIIIIIIIIII

Instructions:

Very common in a lot of South America is to drink 'Mate' (mah-tay, not mate!), which is a sort of loose leaf green tea. Try it, allowing the whole neighborhood to share and drink from the same cup and straw for true authenticity.

1) Melt the lard in a pan and then stir in the turmeric powder.

2) Mix the flour and sugar with a pinch or 2 of salt and then pour in the melted lard mixture. Crumb together until you have a fine crumb.

3) Mound the crumbs into an almost 'volcano' – a mound with a well in the top. Add in a cup of warm water, little by little, whilst kneading to form a dough.

4) Once the dough is well incorporated and has a smooth, elastic-y texture, cut it into 25 small balls of equal size. Leave them to rest overnight, covered with a towel.

5) Peel and dice the potatoes and allow them to boil for 5 minutes and then drain

6) Dice the onions and add them to a pan with the oil.

7) Dice the beef and add it to the onions, along with the stock. Leave the mixture to simmer for 10 minutes. Once the meat is almost tender, add in the potatoes, along with the parsley, oregano, chili and raisins and simmer for a further 2 minutes.

8) Stir in the gelatin and then remove from the heat. Cover and refrigerate overnight.

9) The next day, chill the dough for 30 minutes and preheat oven to 500°F.

10) Roll the dough out into rounds. They will be around 15 cm across and less than 1 cm in thickness.

11) Take the filling which will now be almost 'set,' and place a heaps Tbsp.ful in the centre.

12) Wet the edges along the outside of the dough and fold it over in half. Use your fingers or a fork to firmly press the edges to seal tightly.

13) Line a baking tray with parchment paper, and place the salteñas with the joined edge facing upwards onto it. Beat the egg and brush over the pastry. Bake for 8-10, invites until the outside is crunchy.

14) Leave them to sit for at least 5 minutes before serving.

Tips: When each salteña is ready, place it back in the refrigerator to keep it cool before cooking.

The broth should re-melt in the cooking process, so ensure that the edges are properly sealed and that the dough is thick enough so that moisture won't be leaking out.

(10) Spain - Tortilla

Probably the country's most famous dish (forgetting paella!), the humble tortilla is simple and delicious and a great choice for a filling and healthy breakfast. Needing one pan and only the most basic of ingredients, we know you're about to start a Spanish love affair with this dish.

Yield: 6

Cooking Time: 35 minutes

Ingredient List:

- 12 ¼ oz. potatoes
- 10 eggs
- 3 ½ oz. green olives
- 3 ¼ fl oz. milk
- 2 sprigs rosemary
- 2 garlic cloves
- 1 Tbsp. thyme
- 1 sprig thyme
- 1 red onion
- 1 red pepper
- 1 courgette
- 1 oz. Parmesan
- Olive oil for frying
- Pinch of salt
- Pinch of black pepper

||||||||||||||||||||||||||||||||||||||||||||||||||||||||||

Instructions:

Serve hot and with a selection of European meats and cheeses.

1) Peel the potatoes and then cut into ½ cm thick slices. Boil them for 5 minutes. Then drain and leave to one side.

2) Wash and chop the onion, pepper, garlic and courgette. Also, remove the herb leaves and roughly chop.

3) Heat the olive oil in a large, deep pan. Add the onion, pepper, courgette and the herbs. After 10 minutes, also add the garlic.

4) Whisk together the eggs, milk, Parmesan and parsley with salt and pepper to preference.

5) Chop the olives. Then, stir them into the vegetable mix with the drained potatoes.

6) Pour the egg mixture evenly over the vegetables and leave to cool. Check after 12-15 minutes, and if the bottom is golden brown, flip in to color the other side.

Tips: To flip the tortilla, unless you have flipping skills, tip the pan upside down so that the tortilla slides onto a plate. Then alone it back in with what was the top side now at the bottom.

Keep the heat low-medium to avoid the bottom sticking.

(11) Brazil – Pão de Queijo

Just allow the name of this recipe to marinate in your mind for a second… 'pão de queijo' hails from Brazil (and we very much love pronouncing it in our best Portuguese). The literal translation, ready for this, is cheese bread. You read that right. This is cheese bread. So simple, but incredibly yummy and more-ish. The recipe has been adapted from the traditional ingredients because some are not easy to acquire outside of Brazil, but this version is very close.

Yield: 30

Cooking Time: 35 minutes

Ingredient List:

- 6 Tbsp. olive oil
- 4 cups tapioca flour
- 2 eggs
- 1 ½ cups grated Parmesan
- 1 ¼ cups milk
- 1 cup shredded mozzarella
- Pinch of salt

||||||||||||||||||||||||||||||||||||||||||||||||||||||||||||||

Instructions:

Whilst these are amazing on their own, try your hand at a simple Chimichurri, traditional in Argentina and Brazil, to accompany your bread. It's essentially a mix of chopped garlic, red pepper, chilli pepper and parsley in olive oil and it is divine.

1) Preheat the oven to 400°F. Line a baking tray with parchment paper.

2) In a saucepan on medium heat, combine the milk and oil with ½ cup water and a pinch of salt.

3) Once the mixture has come to the boil, pour it over the tapioca flour and mix well. This mixture will be very sticky.

4) Add the eggs one at a time and keep mixing.

5) Then, add the cheeses little by little until all is mixed.

6) Once everything is incorporated, shape the dough into balls, slightly smaller than a golf ball. You can just use a spoon to scoop some of the mix out and then roll it in your hands into a roughly circular shape.

7) Bake for 15-20 minutes until the balls are puffed and golden brown in color.

Tips: When rolling the balls, have your hands wet with a little cold water to avoid the dough sticking to you.

If possible, use an electric mixer on a low setting – just to save your arm muscles! The mixture gets very sticky so needs quite a bit of power to cut through it.

(12) Russia - Blini

Russian blinis are adorable miniature pancakes, traditionally made of buckwheat. If you've been at any grandiose dinner parties within the last few years, you'll probably have noticed some caviar-topped blini circling as canapés. Well, we say, serve the, for breakfast. Topped with sour cream and smoked salmon these are a refined and delicious savory breakfast option.

Yield: 30

Cooking Time: 20 minutes + 3 hours resting time

Ingredient List:

- 8 oz. smoked salmon
- 6 oz. sour cream
- 5 fl oz. milk
- 5 oz. buckwheat flour
- 2 eggs
- 2 tsp. caraway seeds
- 1 lemon
- 1 cup rocket
- ¾ oz. butter
- ¾ tsp. yeast
- Pinch of salt

IIIIIIIIIIIIIIIIIIIIIIIIIIIIIIIIIIIIIIIIIIIIIIIIIIII

Instructions:

This is a recipe for miniatures. Have a couple for breakfast, or do as the other half do and serve at a dinner party!

1) Pour the milk into a pan until it boils. Separate the eggs whilst you're waiting.

2) Once the milk is boiling, stir in the yeast and then the egg yolks and sour cream.

3) Into a separate bowl, add the flour, caraway seeds and a pinch of salt. Then pour the milk mixture over the top. Stir well and then leave the yeast to ferment for approximately an hour.

4) Whisk the egg whites and then fold them in. Leave the mixture for a further 2 hours.

5) Melt the butter in a pan and then fry the blini a tsp.ful at a time.

6) These are usually served cold. So, once cooled, add a dollop of sour cream on top, along with a slice of smoked salmon and a sprinkle of a rocket. Finally, squeeze in a little lemon juice and enjoy.

Tips: For a vegetarian option, top with spring onion in place of the salmon.

When frying, keep on one side until the bubbles have risen to the top and popped, you can flip it to cook the other side.

(13) China – Jin Dui

Probably known to the majority of us not educated enough to speak Chinese as 'sesame balls,' these self-contained little bites are China's answer to fried donuts and are perfect for a quick breakfast snack on the run! Whilst not necessarily traditionally a breakfast food, these are yummy at any time of day and lend themselves to being a good morning snack.

Yield: 30

Cooking Time: 25 minutes

Ingredient List:

- 10 ½ oz. glutinous rice flour
- 6 oz. red bean paste (or peanut butter for a more Westernized version)
- 2/3 cup white sesame seeds
- ½ cup white sugar
- Oil for frying (roughly 30 fl oz., maybe less depending on the size of your wok)

||||||||||||||||||||||||||||||||||||||||||||||||||||||||||||

Instructions:

Depending on your tastes, if you prefer sweet or savory, you can dip the balls either into a little soy sauce, or blitz up some sesame seeds with a little water and honey to make a sweet sesame dipping sauce.

1) Dissolve the sugar in a ¾ cup of warm water.

2) Combine the sugar water and rice flour and knead into a dough. Add a little extra water or flour as needed to make a moist but firm dough.

3) Divide into 3 equal-sized pieces and roll into balls.

4) Flatten each ball and spoon in a little red bean paste or peanut butter. Wrap the dough back up and roll again into a ball.

5) Quickly dip each ball into a bowl of cold water and the roll in the sesame seeds to coat the outside.

6) Heat enough oil in a wok or deep pan to be able to cover the balls fully.

7) Once the oil is heated, but not spitting, carefully drop in the balls. Use a spoon to turn them so that they cook evenly. Once the sesame balls have turned a golden color, remove from the oil and drain the excess oil off on a paper towel before serving.

Tips: Heat the oil on a high heat but lower the temperature before using it for frying. This reduces spitting at you, which will mean that it hurts less! Also, it means the balls are more likely to cook through rather than just crisp quickly on the outside and stay raw inside.

Make sure that the dough is properly sealed up around the filling to avoid the mixture leaking out during frying.

(14) Philippines – Champorado

Whilst in the last few decades, other places have been discovering chocolate cereals, the Filipinos have been doing it right all along! This traditional dish can rightly be called the original chocolate cereal, and once you taste it, you'll see that it has rightfully earned such a title.

Yield: 4

Cooking Time: 15 minutes

Ingredient List:

- 8 Tbsp. cocoa powder
- 1 ½ cups glutinous rice (this is grown in South Asia. If unavailable, regular rice will do as a substitute)
- 2/3 cup sweetened condensed milk
- ½ cup sugar
- ½ cup coconut milk
- ½ tsp. vanilla extract

||||||||||||||||||||||||||||||||||||||||||||||||||||||||

Instructions:

Serve hot or chill in cute little mason jars if you're okay with cold rice pudding (I know some people aren't!)

1) Cook the rice in a pan of water, adding double the quantity of water to rice. The water can be room temperature and doesn't need to be pre-boiled.

2) Keep stirring the rice until it thickens and has taken on a lot of the water.

3) Add in the cocoa powder, coconut milk, sugar and vanilla extract. You can add more cocoa powder for bitterness or more sugar for sweetness to taste.

4) Remove from the heat once the water is absorbed and all ingredients have been incorporated.

5) Serve with a swirl of condensed milk on top.

Tips: You can change up the consistency, based on personal preference. If you like it a little more liquid-y, add in the coconut milk at the end. Alternatively, take off the heat a little earlier to achieve a stickier result.

If you don't have so much of a sweet tooth, leave the sugar out of the rice mix and simply serve with a dash of the condensed milk. The bitterness of the cocoa will come through a lot stronger without the sugar.

(15) Colombia – Arepas

Arepas are a true Colombian staple, served with every meal. This arepa is 'de queso.' The saltiness of the cheese and the sweetness of the arepa dough make a delicious mouthful in every bite.

Yield: 6

Cooking Time: 5 minutes

Ingredient List:

- 5 Tbsp. plain flour
- 3 Tbsp. butter
- 2 cups Colombian cheese (this is a white, crumbly cheese. You could substitute in feta or something similar if the real, Colombian stuff is unavailable)
- 2 cups yellow cornmeal (pre-cooked)
- 2 Tbsp. sugar
- ½ cup milk
- Pinchó of salt

|||||||||||||||||||||||||||||||||||||||||||||||||||||||||||||

Instructions:

If you have a savory-sweet palette, then you can add a little-fried pineapple in the centre with the cheese for some extra added sweetness.

1) Knead together the flour, butter, cornmeal and sugar with 1 ½ cups of warm water. Add a pinch of salt.

2) Split the dough into 12 balls of equal size. Then place the balls on a lined baking tray and with another layer of greaseproof paper. Use another baking tray on top and press down to flatten the balls down to about 1/8 of an inch thickness.

3) Divide the cheese evenly between 6 of the rounds. Then, top each one with the remaining 6. Seal the edges with a little water and your fingers.

4) Melt the butter in a pan. Then use it to fry the arepas, 3 minutes on each side, until they have become crispy and golden brown.

Tips: When kneading, keep moistening your hands with water to keep your dough moist and well-combined.

When forming the balls, try to keep the dough smooth and without cracks. This is because when frying, cracks will be magnified and may cause your arepa to spilt open.

(16) Oman – Khabeesa

Oh man – what I wouldn't do for some traditional khabeesa, straight from Oman! A middle-eastern mix of sweet flavours and spices adorn this dish of farina resembling porridge. A good bowl of kahbeese in the morning will be sure to see you all the way through to lunchtime.

Yield: 4-6

Cooking Time: 20 minutes

Ingredient List:

- 3 ½ cups milk
- 2 Tbsp. rose water
- 2 Tbsp. butter
- 1 ½ cups condensed milk
- 1 Tbsp. cardamom
- 2/3 cup farina
- ½ cup desiccated coconut
- ½ cup pistachios
- ½ cup dates
- ½ tsp. saffron
- ¼ cup sesame seeds

||||||||||||||||||||||||||||||||||||||||||||||||||||||||

Instructions:

This is already a filling and yummy breakfast, but you could top with additional all fresh and dried fruits to add some extra vitamins and fiber to make this even better for you.

1) On medium heat, combine the milk with the farina, cardamom, and saffron.

2) Once the mix is simmering, add in the condensed milk and rose water and reduce to a low heat. Allow the mix to simmer for 10 minutes.

3) Melt the butter and chop the pistachios and dates.

4) Serve in bowls and top with a drizzle of butter, pistachios, dates, sesame seeds and coconut.

Tips: If farina is difficult to find where you are, you can switch it out for semolina.

Depending on how much of a rose water fan you are, adding it in earlier or later will affect the strength of its flavour. If you're looking for a really big rose water hit, add it in at the last minute before removing from the heat.

(17) Costa Rica – Gallo Pinto

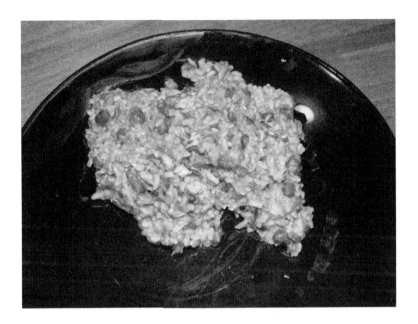

Whilst it only refers to the ride and beans part of the dish, we have included pico de gallo and fried plantain and egg too, as it's traditionally eaten with as part of a delicious Costa Rican breakfast.

Yield: 6

Cooking Time: 35 minutes

Ingredient List:

- 30 oz. cooked, canned black beans
- 6 eggs
- 3 garlic cloves
- 3 cups rice
- 2 ripe plantains
- 2 tomatoes
- 2 onions
- 2 avocados
- 1 1/4 cup chopped cilantro
- 1 red pepper
- 1 cup spring onions
- ½ a jalapeño
- ¼ tsp. cinnamon
- Pinch of salt
- Pinch of black pepper
- Olive oil for frying

Instructions:

This breakfast would traditionally be served with fresh Costa Rican coffee, or fresh juice, make from one of the huge selection of exotic fruits native to the country, such as pineapple, watermelon or passion fruit.

1) Cook the rice in 6 cups of water in a pan. Cover the pan and leave for 12 minutes. Then check and remove from heat once the water is all cooked in. Take care that the bottom hasn't stuck.

2) Meanwhile, dice the garlic and dice the rest of the vegetables into the small chunks. The plantain cooks best in 1-2 inch thick slices, cut diagonally.

3) For the pico de gallo, toss together the tomato, jalapeño, 1 onion, half of the spring onion and ½ a cup of cilantro.

4) Sauté the remaining onion along with the garlic and red pepper in a little olive oil. Add this to the cooked rice.

5) Drain the beans and add them to the rice too. Stir well and add in the rest of the cilantro and spring onions and season with salt and pepper to taste.

6) Toss the chopped plantain in the cinnamon. Shallow fry in a pan, turning every 2 minutes until the slices are soft and caramelized. Sprinkle a little salt on both sides of each slice.

7) Finally, fry the eggs to your personal preference. I always suggest keying the yolk runny so that it mixes with the other things on the plate.

8) Serve everything all together on one yummy plate – gallo pinto (the rice and beans), pico de gallo (the tomato salsa), the plantain, a fried egg and some avocado. ¡Qué rico!

Tips: Traditionally, this dish is made with the rice and beans leftover from the day before (they are a staple for breakfast, lunch, and dinner). So, for more authenticity, cook your rice the day before.

If you are a fan of sweet and savory, try some brown sugar in with the cinnamon to toss the plantains in. It is the yummiest way to eat them, but it's down to personal preference whether you would want something so sweet with a savory dish.

(18) Nigeria – Plantain Mosa

So we thought you might like a fried taste of Africa. Plantain is a delicious staple over a lot of the continent, and in this classic Nigerian dish, the plantain is made into a 'puff' and fried, which is scientifically proven to make everything taste better!

Yield: 16

Cooking Time: 30 minutes

Ingredient List:

- 4 Tbsp. plain flour
- 2 tsp. yeast
- 1 ripe plantain
- ¾ tsp. cayenne pepper
- Pinch of salt
- Oil for frying

|||||||||||||||||||||||||||||||||||||||||||||||||||||||

Instructions:

Use there as a savory or sweet breakfast option. For savory, a spicy tomato salsa would work nicely. If you're more sweet-toothed, you can easily scoop on some Nutella, or eat with fruit.

1) In a deep pan, begin heating the oil for frying. You want it to be at least 3 inches deep.

2) Mix the yeast with 8 Tbsp. of warm water and set aside.

3) Peel and mash the plantain.

4) Add the yeast mix into the flour and add a pinch of salt. Stir well.

5) Next, stir in the plantain too. If the consistency appears to be too thick, add a little extra water. If it's too thin, add extra flour a little at a time.

6) Cover the mixture with foil or cling wrap and allow to sit for 10-15 minutes.

7) Next, beat the batter and add the pepper.

8) Test the temperature of the oil with a small drop of the batter. The oil should sizzle, and the batter will rise quickly to the top. If it's correct, use an ice cream scoop to drop balls of the batter into the oil. Using this size should yield 16 balls. Use a spoon to keep turning the balls so that they get fried evenly.

9) Once golden brown, transfer the balls into a sieve or colander lined with paper towels to drain excess oil.

Tips: If you have a deep fat fryer, you can use it. However, still take plenty of care to turn the balls so that they giver cooked evenly.

Adding the spice is the traditional Nigerian way, however, if you want to adapt into a sweet version, substitute the cayenne for cinnamon.

(19) Egypt – Ful Medames & Tahini

Ful Medames, a dish of fava beans, is actually Egypt's national dish, which means that it's eaten pretty much all day, every day, and therefore is a prime candidate for a North African breakfast. An old Arab saying claims that "Beans have satisfied even the Pharaohs." Well, if it's good enough for them, then we have to give it a go!

Yield: 4

Cooking Time: 180 minutes

Ingredient List:

- 5 cloves of garlic
- 4 eggs
- 4 Tbsp. extra virgin olive oil
- 3 lemons
- 2 large tomatoes
- 2 cups small fava beans
- 1 cup sesame seeds
- 1 Tbsp. chilli flakes
- 1 Tbsp. cumin
- ½ a cucumber
- 1/3 cup chopped parsley
- 1/3 cup cilantro
- Pinch of salt
- Pinch of black pepper

||||||||||||||||||||||||||||||||||||||||||||||||||||||

Instructions:

We haven't included the recipe for a homemade version here, but if you could serve with some traditional Arab flatbread to mop up the juices, your taste buds and your full stomach will both be thanking you!

1) We'll start with making the tahini, since this can be done in a larger quantity to use in other things (in hummus, as a sauce for kebabs, or sweetened with honey and spread on toast), and can be made ahead of time and kept in the refrigerator. Heat a pan to medium and toast the sesame seeds, tossing and constantly stirring as they burn easily. Once they've started to brown, transfer them to a food processor. Add the olive oil and a pinch of salt and black pepper to taste. Blend into a paste, and there you have it!

2) Now onto the ful medames. First, we need to cook the beans. Pour them into a saucepan and simmer them in water for 2 and a half hours. Keep checking back for the first 2 hours and adding more water so that they are always fully covered. Once the beans are softened, take a ladle out and mash them, before adding back into the pan. Mix in the garlic, cumin, chilli, and salt. The beans can be kept warm on a low heat whilst you prepare the rest of the garnishes.

3) Hard boil the eggs by having them in a saucepan of boiling water for 9 minutes, and then de-shell and quarter them.

4) Make a salsa by dicing the tomato and cucumber and mixing in the cilantro and the juice of one lemon.

5) Serve the beans and crop with the chopped parsley. Serve alongside the eggs and a little of the tomato salsa, and a dressing of the tahini sauce.

Tips: This recipe is pretty time-consuming, and if we're looking at breakfast, it's likely that you don't have a lot of time in the morning, right? The good news is that pretty much everything can be prepared a day ahead of time so that it's ready to be served up for breakfast. The only thing to make fresh, if possible, will be the tomato salsa.

Have additional salt, pepper, lemon and garlic available for your diners to season according to personal taste.

(20) Netherlands – Ontbitjkoek

Literally translated from Dutch, this much-loved breakfast item is 'breakfast cake.' Yes, those are 2 words that should always go together! Almost a Dutch take in gingerbread, this cake is a dark mix of spices which will leave you with the delightful aroma of a European bakery for a long time.

Yield: 8

Cooking Time: 75 minutes + overnight dough resting

Ingredient List:

- 3 cups rye flour
- 3 Tbsp. brown sugar
- 1 Tbsp. baking powder
- 1 tsp. cardamom
- 1 tsp. cinnamon
- ¾ Tbsp. honey
- ½ cup white sugar
- ½ tsp. ginger
- ¼ tsp. cloves
- ¼ tsp. black pepper
- ¼ tsp. nutmeg
- Pinch of coriander seeds
- Pinch of aniseed
- Pinch of salt

||||||||||||||||||||||||||||||||||||||||||||||||||||||||

Instructions:

Traditionally, this is sliced like bread and buttered on one side. Also, apparently the Dutch are major fans on peanut butter so go ahead and spread some of that on too!

1) Stir together the flour, baking powder, brown sugar, all of the spices and a pinch of salt.

2) In a saucepan, boil together the white sugar, honey and ½ cup of water.

3) Then, in an electric mixer because the sugar mix is hot, mix the sugar and dry ingredients to form a dough. Once it's cooled a little, you can use your hands to knead the dough for a further few minutes.

4) Line a loaf tin with greaseproof paper and pour in the mixture evenly. Cling wrap the top and leave it to stand overnight.

5) Once the dough has rested for more than 12 hours, preheat the oven to 340°F.

Bake for 45-60 minutes, checking that there is a firmer crust on top and that the middle is cooked but still moist.

Tips: Taste the dough before pouring into the loaf tin to check that the spice mix is right for you. During cooking, the flours will soften a little, so bear that in mind, but feel free to adjust to your taste.

This dough will be dark, do take care to test it with a skewer test before removing from the oven, not just assuming that it's done because the top is dark.

(21) England – The Fry Up

Prepare your arteries and take a seat for this mega-breakfast from this author's homeland, England. Take many firm favourite breakfasts items; egg, bacon, bread, potatoes… and fry them all! Your plate will most likely be dripping with grease, but that's okay! Just take another piece of bread and mop it up!

Yield: 2

Cooking Time: 25-35 minutes

Ingredient List:

- 24 ½ oz. haricot beans
- 24 ½ oz. chopped tinned tomatoes
- 4 rashers bacon, smoked
- 4 eggs
- 3 Tbsp. butter
- 2 potatoes
- 2 medium tomatoes
- 2 sausages
- 2 slices white bread
- 1 cup mushrooms
- 1 tsp. English mustard
- 1 tsp. muscovado sugar
- 1 tsp. vinegar
- 1 clove garlic
- 1 onion
- Pinch of salt
- Pinch of black pepper

Instructions:

No matter where you are in the world, I urge you to enjoy this like a real Brit. You will need a strong cup of English tea and squeeze bottles of both tomato ketchup and brown sauce on hand.

1) Chop the onion and garlic small and pop in a saucepan will a dash of oil to soften for about 5 minutes. Only use half of the onion.

2) Pour in the chopped tomatoes, along with the mustard, sugar, vinegar and a pinch of salt. Allow this to simmer for a few minutes to incorporate before adding the beans. Taste the sauce and season to your preference. Leave the mixture simmering on a low heat until you have finished prepare everything else and there you will have your very own, homemade baked beans!

3) Next, we'll prepare our also homemade hash browns. Peel the potatoes and shred them into a large bowl of cold water. Once water is cloudy, drain and place the shredded potato into a new bowl of water. Repeat the process again, this time, not adding more water but patting the potato dry with a paper towel. Stir the remaining onion into the potato mixture. Season with salt and pepper to your preference.

4) In a large pan, melt the butter. Then, using round cookie cutters if you have metal ones, and otherwise making the shape roughly yourself. Place the potato mix into 4 rounds and cook for about 7 minutes, until a crust has formed on the bottom. At this point, or when the hash browns look stable enough, flip them over to crisp up the other side too.

5) Unfortunately, unless you're a farmer and a butcher, the rest of the elements we cannot really home make. You will need to cook the bacon and sausages according to the package instructions.

6) With tour fresh tomatoes, slice each into 3 parts. Trim and chop the mushrooms too. In a pan, add a dash of oil and place in the mushrooms. After 3 minutes, place your tomatoes slices in carefully too. Fry both of these up to your personal preference.

7) Each plate will also need 2 fried eggs. Take a pan and add only a small amount of oil. Keep it on a low heat and crack your eggs into the pan. When the white is no longer translucent, they're done. Sprinkle a pinch of salt onto the yolks. You can then flip them over to further cook the yolk if you like it firmer.

8) The last thing to do will be to toast your bread and put your magnificent breakfast feasts onto a plate.

Tips: Since we have a lot of elements and, unless you own a restaurant, you probably won't have enough hob space to cook gem all at once, you can turn the oven on to a very low heat setting and keep the already cooked elements warm in the oven until you're ready to serve.

Whilst it's true that the camp is divided when it comes to runny vs. firm yolks, please allow me to very much advise you to go runny for this one. The yolk running all over your plate will add moisture and tie in all of the elements together.

(22) Malta - Qagħaq ta'l-għasel

I'm going to hazard a guess that unless you are one of Malta's 450,000 residents, you probably don't speak Maltese. If so, here's a yummy surprise for you. Qagħaq ta'l-għasel are essentially delicious little treacle cookies. We are by no means confining these to morning snacking, but they sure do make a yummy breakfast on the run.

Yield: 16

Cooking Time: 40 minutes + overnight refrigeration

Ingredient List:

- 17 ½ oz. plain flour
- 15 ¾ oz. treacle
- 8 ¾ oz. semolina
- 3 ½ oz. sugar
- 3 Tbsp. orange marmalade
- 2 Tbsp. cocoa powder
- 1 ¾ oz. butter
- 1 egg
- 1 lemon
- 1 orange
- 1 tsp. nutmeg
- 1 tsp. cinnamon
- 1 tsp. cloves

||||||||||||||||||||||||||||||||||||||||||||||||||||||||

Instructions:

These little treats literally taste of Christmas. Serve with something festive and winter-y, such as a mulled wine or some eggnog.

1) Grate the rinds off of the orange and lemon.

2) In a pan over medium heat, pour in 13 ½ fl oz. of water and combine with the treacle, sugar, marmalade, cocoa powder, rinds, and spices. Stir continually until the mixture reaches the boil.

3) Reduce the temperature to low and slowly add the semolina, stirring continuously.

4) Remove from the heat once the semolina is cooked. The mixture should be smooth, not gritty and will take approximately 10 minutes.

5) Crumb together the butter and flour.

6) Juice the orange and add this to the breadcrumbs, along with the egg. Add in up to 3 ½ fl oz. of water if needed to combine everything into a soft dough and knead.

7) Refrigerate both components overnight.

8) Preheat the oven to 350°F and line a baking tray with greaseproof paper.

9) Cut the pastry into 16 even pieces. Roll each piece into a long and fairly thin rectangle, but still wide enough that the sides can be folded over to meet each other.

10) Spoon some of the treacle filling along the centre of each piece of dough and fold the dough over to meet itself. Roll into more of a round, sausage shape, and then join the 2 ends together to make a hoop.

11) With a sharp knife, make some small slits in the dough and pull these open slightly to reveal the filling.

12) Arrange the rings in the baking tray and bake for 15-20 minutes until they are just starting to color on top.

Tips: To add even more warmth into these winter-y treats, add a splash of almond liquor into the filling mix to taste.

Don't roll the pastry too thin, or the filling will be too heavy for it and ooze out.

(23) Finland – Karjalan Piirakka

Time for a taste of Northern Europe now, a place famous for incredible snowy winters, cool cities and… pickled herring?! I wish no offense to anyone who's a fan of such a delicacy, but it's certainly not for me. So instead, I've found another offering for you from Finland, a traditional savory baked pastry.

Yield: 16

Cooking Time: 50 minutes

Ingredient List:

- 2 cups milk
- 2 eggs
- 1 cup rice
- 1 cup rye flour
- 1 cup butter
- ¼ cup plain flour
- ¼ tsp. ground ginger
- Pinch of salt
- Pinch of pepper

||||||||||||||||||||||||||||||||||||||||||||||||||||||||||

Instructions:

If you're a cheese freak, which, let's be honest, a lot of us are, then just before serving, grate a little cheese on top and microwave for just 10 seconds to melt it down a little.

1) Bring the rice to the boil with 2 cups of water.

2) After 10 minutes or so, when the rice has absorbed most but not all of the water, add in the milk too. Stir frequently until the rice has taken on the moisture and is now creamy in texture. Remove from the heat and set aside.

3) Place the eggs into a hard boil. You can leave them for 8-10 minutes and then they should be ready.

4) Preheat the oven to 450°F and line a baking tray with greaseproof paper.

5) Now to prepare the pastry. Combine both of the flours with ½ cup of water, also adding a pinch of salt. Do not add extra water as this dough needs to be stiff.

6) Lightly flour a surface and cut the dough into 16 equal pieces. Then, roll each piece into a circle, roughly 6 inches across.

7) In the centre of each round, place the filling. You should have enough for about 3 Tbsp. in each.

8) Fold the dyes over to cover the filling partway, leaving the middle exposed. Using your fingers, creating a crimping pattern along the edges.

9) Melt 1/3 cup butter and brush over the pastries. Then bake for 10-15 minutes, until the edges of the pastries are browning.

10) Whilst the pastries are cooking, you can make the 'egg butter' topping. Remove the egg shells and chop the eggs into small pieces. Cream the remaining butter and then stir in the chopped egg. Season to taste with the salt, pepper, and ginger.

11) Allow the pastries to cool and then serve along with the 'egg butter.'

Tips: If you find that the pastry crust is a little hard, which may well happen with such a dry pastry, place them in a ziplock bag for a couple of hours before the cool.

Rice is just one traditional filling. You could also try with mashed potatoes or pickled fish.

(24) Madagascar – Malagasy Cake

'Malagasy' refers to a group of cuisine from Madagascar as a whole, drawing on influences from many of the cultures of the island's historical settlers, and combining them with some of the fantastic produce grown in Madagascar. We thought you might like something yummy and sweet so here is a traditional Malagasy cake for you.

Yield: 4

Cooking Time: 30 minutes

Ingredient List:

- 4 overripe bananas
- 4 eggs
- 4 Tbsp. sugar
- 3 ½ oz. grated cassava
- 2 cups milk
- 2 Tbsp. cream
- 1 vanilla pod
- ½ oz. butter
- ½ tsp. nutmeg
- ½ tsp. cloves

|||||||||||||||||||||||||||||||||||||||||||||||||||||||||

Instructions:

Given the theme of the book, we suggest that you enjoy some of this cake for breakfast! Serve with some fresh berries, or some of Madagascar's finest, such as pineapple, papaya, and passion fruit.

1) Preheat the oven to 350°F and line a small baking tray with greaseproof paper.

2) In a pan, bring the milk, vanilla pod, sugar, cloves and nutmeg to boiling point.

3) Lower the heat and add in the cassava. Cook on low for 10 minutes, stirring every so often.

4) Remove from the heat. Take out the vanilla pod and then stir in the cream.

5) Mash the bananas and add them to the mix.

6) Stir in the eggs, one at a time.

7) Bake for 12-15 minutes, until a skewer can be inserted and come out clean.

Tips: There is not a lot of sugar in this recipe. The sweetness will mainly come from the ripe bananas. The riper they are, they sweeter they'll be, so don't be afraid to leave your bananas to get almost entirely black, as you'll be mashing them anyway!

Change up and add the spices to fit your personal taste. Cinnamon or allspice would also work well.

(25) France – Croissants & Pains au Chocolat

As one of the coolest and most suave European countries, France is a place where dessert for breakfast is allowed. (Sorry for the upcoming stereotype) Dress in a striped shirt, don a beret and sit alone, mysteriously, enjoying (possibly imaginary) views of L'Arc de Triomphe and L'Torre Eiffel and chowing down on some delicious French pastries. We've split the recipes so that if you don't have time to make both, you can choose just the one you want.

Yield: 6 of each pastry

Cooking Time: 90 minutes + at least 6 hours chilling

Ingredient List:

- Croissants: Pains at Chocolat:
- 3 ¾ oz. plain flour 8 ¾ oz. plain flour
- 2 ¾ fl oz. milk 6 ¼ oz. butter
- 2 ½ oz. butter 4 ½ oz. dark chocolate
- 1 ¼ tsp. caster sugar 1 ½ oz. caster sugar
- 1 egg 1 egg
- ¾ tsp. yeast ½ tsp. yeast
- Pinch of salt pinch of salt

||||||||||||||||||||||||||||||||||||||||||||||||||||||

Instructions:

Pastries are always even more delectable when served fresh and warm. Oh, and also with fresh coffee too.

1) Croissants – Mix the yeast with ¼ tsp. sugar and stir into 1 ½ Tbsp. warm water. Leave it to sit for 5 minutes until the mixture is frothy on top. Heat the milk in the microwave, and then pour it over the remaining sugar and a pinch of salt. Then, stir in the flour and the yeast mix, until everything combines to form a dough. Cling wrap the bowl, and leave the dough to rise until it's tripled in volume. Remove the cling wrap for another 10 minutes and then cling again until the dough has doubled in size again. Remove the wrap and chill the dough for 20 minutes. Have the butter chilling. Roll out the dough into a rectangle, about 2 cm thick. Allow the butter to warm a little, and then spread over the top 2 thirds of the rectangle. Fold the unbuttered third up over the middle, and then the top third over the top too, so that you now have 3 layers. Turn the dough 90° and then roll out and repeat the fold in motion again. Place the dough into a ziplock bag and refrigerate for 2 hours. Then, sprinkle the dough with flour and repeat the rolling and folding. Replace the dough in the bag and refrigerate for another 2 hours. Next, roll out the dough into a rectangle about 1 cm thick.

Cut into 3 equal squares and cut each square into 2 triangles. Taking the base of the triangle, loosely roll it up to form the croissant. Allow another 2 hours for the dough to rise more. Preheat the oven to 460°F and line a baking tray with greaseproof paper. Egg wash the pastry and bake for 15-20 minutes, until golden brown.

2) Pains au Chocolat – Mix the flour, sugar, yeast and a pinch of salt together along with 4 ½ fl oz. water. It will come together to form a dough. Once this happens, knead for 5 minutes. Chill the butter, and then allow it to come up in temperature just a little so that you can roll it out into a 1 cm thick rectangle. Roll the dough into a rectangle 1 ½ times the size of the butter. Place the butter rectangle so that it covers the top 2 thirds of the dough. Fold the non-buttered third up and over the middle section, and then pull the top third down to cover it. Roll out the dough gently, just to press down the layers onto each other and then place in a zip lock bag to chill for 20 minutes. Roll the dough out into a rectangle again and repeat the folding in thirds process. Chill again and repeat the rolling, folding and chilling process another 2 times and then wrap and chill for at least 2 hours. Preheat the oven to 430°F. Roll the dough out to a 1 cm thick rectangle and then cut into 6 equally sized squares. If the chocolate is in squares, break into 6 even parts. If not, roughly chop and

weigh it out into 6 even parts. Arrange the chocolate along one edge of the square, and then fold the dough over it to make a kind of sausage. Flatten the top a little. Place the pastries on a baking tray lines with greaseproof paper, and egg wash the top. Leave for another hour to allow the dough to rise a little more, then bake for 15-20 minutes until golden brown.

Tips: With this kind of pastry especially, it often works out much better if it's kept cold throughout the process. Don't be afraid to re-chill at any point if it's coming up to room temperature.

Once you have this type of pastry down, you can try your hand at some other French classics, such as Pains au Raisins (always add a splash of Cognac for good measure) or Almond 'Danish' pastries.

(26) Lithuania - Grybukai

So these are adorable little Latvian mushroom cookies! No, they're not made of many rooms, they're just shaped and decorated to look like them. Adorable, right? These take quite a bit of time and effort, and so these are more of a special occasion breakfast treat. Whenever you decide it's time to try your hand at these little cuties, we know you're going love them.

Yield: 30

Cooking Time: 75 minutes + overnight and 8 hours setting times

Ingredient List:

- 4 eggs
- 2 2/3 cups icing sugar
- 2 ½ cups plain flour
- 2 cups uncooked rice
- 2 Tbsp. lemon juice
- 2 tsp. cinnamon
- 1 Tbsp. baking powder
- 1 tsp. nutmeg
- 1 tsp. vanilla extract
- 2/3 cup butter
- 2/3 cup cocoa powder
- 1/3 cup honey
- 1/3 cup molasses
- ¼ cup whole milk
- ¼ cup poppy seeds
- ¼ tsp. cloves
- Pinch of salt

Instructions:

You can leave these in a cool, dry place for a few days before serving to make the most of their naturally crunchy texture.

1) In a saucepan, melt together the milk, honey, molasses and ½ cup of butter.

2) Mix the flour, baking powder, cinnamon, cloves, nutmeg and a pinch of salt.

3) Whisk together 2 of the eggs and 1 Tbsp. of the lemon juice. Then pour this into the butter mix.

4) Gradually stir in the dry ingredients to the butter mix to create a sticky dough. The cover the pan and refrigerate overnight.

5) The next day, preheat the oven to 375°F and line 2 large baking trays with greaseproof paper.

6) Divide the dough into 3 even portions. Take two of the thirds, and out of them, make 30 small balls, shaped to be like the cap of a mushroom. Space them out evenly on the baking sheets.

7) Use the other piece of dough to create 30 'stems.' These should be fairly cylindrical and not too long in length, maybe 2 inches long. Space them out of the baking sheets too.

8) Bake the cookie parts for only 8-10 minutes, until lightly golden brown and hardened.

9) Separate the 2 remaining eggs and whisk together with the other Tbsp. of lemon juice. Beat in 2 cups of the icing sugar until the icing is fairly thick but still able to run.

10) Fill a deep casserole dish with the uncooked rice, leveling it out. Take the 'caps' and, using a sharp paring knife, cut out the middle section, the size to fit in a 'stem.'

11) Paint the underside of each 'cap' with the white icing and also drip some into the centre hole you've just created. Insert a stem into each cap. Place each mushroom 'cap down' into the rice and leave to set at room temperature for at least 4 hours. Meanwhile, cover the bowl of white icing with plastic wrap.

12) Then, paint the stems with the white icing and dip the bottom half into the poppy seeds to resemble the 'mud.' Place the mushrooms back into the rice for another 2 hours.

13) In a pan in low heat, mix the remaining butter and icing sugar, along with the cocoa powder, vanilla extract, a pinch of salt and ¼ cup of water. Whisk until thick and creamy.

14) Whilst the icing is still warm, dip the mushroom caps into the black icing, and then place the mushrooms 'stem down' into the rice, adding more rice if necessary to hold them stable.

Tips: If you are the artistic type, then you could use a tiny amount of beetroot juice or red food colouring to create a red icing for the cap, and paint of white or black spots.

So as to not have to cut a huge hole in the caps, taper the stems into a skinnier point at one end and use that end to insert into the cap.

(27) Greece – Galatopita

Often now viewed as a dessert, we have reliable evidence that galatopita started its life as a deliciously sweet Greek breakfast item. Sometimes it's referred to a 'Greek Milk Pie,' but the Greek word 'galatopita' sounds way better. This recipe is also much simpler than other baked Greek goods which require tricky phyllo pastry, so we're winning all around.

Yield: 8

Cooking Time: 80 minutes

Ingredient List:

- 5 cups milk
- 3 eggs
- 1 cup semolina
- 1 cup sugar
- 1 tsp. cinnamon
- ½ cup butter + extra for greasing
- Icing sugar for dusting

IIIIIIIIIIIIIIIIIIIIIIIIIIIIIIIIIIIIIIIIIIIIIIIIIIIIIIIIII

Instructions:

What could go better with this Greek treat than some natural Greek yoghurt, swirled with honey? Also, top with hazelnuts for some added crunch.

1) Preheat the oven to 350°F.

2) In a pan, heat the milk until it begins to simmer. Then, add in the butter, sugar, cinnamon and semolina, stirring as the mixture thickens.

3) Beat the eggs and add them in as the mixture continues to thicken. You are looking to create a thick cream.

4) Use butter the well grease a cake tin. Then, pour in the mixture.

5) Bake for an hour and then turn off the oven. Leave the pie in for a further 15 minutes as the oven is cooling.

6) Dust the top with icing sugar and extra cinnamon if you wish.

Tips: You can add a coating of coarse sugar on the top, and burn with a blow torch for an almost crème brûlée feel.

This recipe is for a pretty plain custard. If you're looking to jazz things up a little, you could flavor with lemon, orange or honey to keep the Greek flavours.

(28) Jamaica – Green Banana Porridge

This spiced Jamaican take on often boring porridge will knock your socks off! Praised for its ability to keep many stomachs full for hours until the next meal, green banana porridge is a fond childhood memory of many Jamaicans. Tasty, filling and nutritious, there's nothing not to love about this breakfast, so go ahead, give it a go!

Yield: 4

Cooking Time: 25 minutes

Ingredient List:

- 6 unripe (green) bananas
- 1 cup coconut milk
- 1 cup sweetened condensed milk
- 1 tsp. cinnamon
- 1 tsp. vanilla extract
- 1 tsp. lemon juice
- ½ tsp. nutmeg
- ¼ tsp. allspice
- Pinch of salt

||||||||||||||||||||||||||||||||||||||||||||||||||||||||||

Instructions:

Let's really get a taste of the Caribbean and serve with some fresh exotic fruit juice, pineapple or banana would work, or some fresh coconut water.

1) Peel the bananas and chop into small pieces. Drizzle the lemon juice over the top.

2) Combine 1 cup of the coconut milk with one cup of water and blend with the bananas.

3) Pour the banana mix into a saucepan on medium heat.

4) Stir in the spices and a pinch of salt.

5) Continue stirring for 10-15 minutes, allowing the mixture to thicken. Add extra milk if needed, to get to your desired consistency.

6) Add in the vanilla and condensed milk to taste.

Tips: Obviously, you can use riper bananas, but traditionally this dish isn't supposed to be overly sweet, which is why the green bananas are used.

Top with some nuts, seeds and fresh fruit for added nutritional value.

(29) Haiti – Akasan

We all know the struggle. We love breakfast. We really want some breakfast! But you sometimes just don't have the time, or you just can't stomach something hearty to eat. Well, the Haitians understood our struggle too, and that's why they came up with their delicious cornmeal shake, akasan. This shake is perfect for a light something to start the day with or to take on the run.

Yield: 4

Cooking Time: 10 minutes

Ingredient List:

- 12 oz. evaporated milk
- 3 anise stars
- 1 tsp. vanilla extract
- 1 tsp. cinnamon
- ½ cup corn flour
- ¼ cup sugar
- Pinch of salt

||||||||||||||||||||||||||||||||||||||||||||||||||||||

Instructions:

This is served traditionally both warm and cold. You can make a larger batch ahead of time and refrigerate and then serve chilled.

1) Boil together 2 cups of water with a pinch of salt, the sugar, the cinnamon and the star anise.

2) Mix the cornflour with ½ cup of water in a bowl to form a paste.

3) Slowly incorporate the corn flour paste into the boiling water, constantly stirring to eliminate lumps.

4) Turn the heat down to low and leave the mixture to cook for a further 5 minutes.

5) Remove the anise stars and stir in the evaporated milk and vanilla extract. Ensure that everything is well combined and then removes from the heat.

Tips: take care with the stirring to remove any lumps. Nobody wants a lumpy milkshake!

Take this shake to go with some fresh fruit, and you've got yourself a nutritious and balanced start to the day.

(30) Iraq – Kahi & Geymar

You're going to need your sweet tooth for this Iraqi breakfast dish. Here are layers of flaky pastry, drenched is sticky sweet date syrup and topped with geymar, a thick cream made from buffalo milk. If you wanted a sweet, sweet taste of the Middle East, here it is for you on a plate!

Yield: 4

Cooking Time: 60 minutes

Ingredient List:

- 2 cups flour
- 2 cups heavy whipping cream
- 2 cups buffalo milk
- 2 cups pitted Medjool dates
- 1 oz. butter
- Pinch of salt

||||||||||||||||||||||||||||||||||||||||||||||||||||||||

Instructions:

Add in as much of the Middle East as you'd like! Dress up with extra dates, chopped pistachios, pomegranate seeds or honey.

1) The day before you wish to serve, you'll have to prepare your geymar. On a low heat, combine the milk and cream, without stirring. Allow a gentle boil for 30-40 minutes and then remove from heat. You want to avoid condensation but need the mixture covered, so cover the pan with a colander and then a tea towel. Leave the mixture sit at room temperate for 6 hours, then place a lid on the pot and refrigerate overnight.

2) Combine the flour with a pinch of salt and start gradually adding up to ¾ cup water whilst combining and kneading the mix, to end up with dough.

3) Cut the dough into 4 equal pieces and then allow it to rest for 15-20 minutes.

4) Preheat the oven to 430°F.

5) Melt the butter.

6) Roll out your dough to as thin as possible, so that it is almost see-through. Then, using a pastry brush, paint some melted butter over the top and fold the dough in half. Flatten the dough again and repeat. Keep repeating until you have 4 individual pastries, each about 10 cm long.

7) Bake the pastries for 15-25 minutes, until crisped up and golden brown.

8) Whilst the Kahi is baking; you can prepare the date syrup. Chop your dares into small pieces and place them into a pan. Cover them with cold water. Bring to a boil and then reduce to a low heat. Gently bash the dates with a spoon at this point to help the break down further. When you've got a lot of the moisture out, strain the mixture, returning the liquid to the pot. Simmer the liquid until it thickens to the consistency of honey. This will take 10-15 minutes.

9) When you're ready to serve, skim the thick cream off of the top of the Geymar and use that. You can then pour a little of the thinner milk on top if you wish.

Tips: If you're looking to be very authentic, use a cheesecloth or muslin to strain your date syrup.

For those with a sweeter tooth, feel free to sprinkle a little brown sugar in each layer of the pastry.

About the Author

Nancy Silverman is an accomplished chef from Essex, Vermont. Armed with her degree in Nutrition and Food Sciences from the University of Vermont, Nancy has excelled at creating e-books that contain healthy and delicious meals that anyone can make and everyone can enjoy. She improved her cooking skills at the New England Culinary Institute in Montpelier Vermont and she has been working at perfecting her culinary style since graduation. She claims that her life's work is always a work in progress and she only hopes to be an inspiration to aspiring chefs everywhere.

Her greatest joy is cooking in her modern kitchen with her family and creating inspiring and delicious meals. She often says that she has perfected her signature dishes based on her family's critique of each and every one.

Nancy has her own catering company and has also been fortunate enough to be head chef at some of Vermont's most exclusive restaurants. When a friend suggested she share some of her outstanding signature dishes, she decided to add cookbook author to her repertoire of personal achievements. Being a technological savvy woman, she felt the e-book realm would be a better fit and soon she had her first cookbook available online. As of today, Nancy has sold over 1,000 e-books and has shared her culinary experiences and brilliant recipes with people from all over the world! She plans on expanding into self-help books and dietary cookbooks, so stayed tuned!

Author's Afterthoughts

Thank you for making the decision to invest in one of my cookbooks! I cherish all my readers and hope you find joy in preparing these meals as I have.

There are so many books available and I am truly grateful that you decided to buy this one and follow it from beginning to end.

I love hearing from my readers on what they thought of this book and any value they received from reading it. As a personal favor, I would appreciate any feedback you can give in the form of a review on Amazon and please be honest! This kind of support will help others make an informed choice on and will help me tremendously in producing the best quality books possible.

My most heartfelt thanks,

Nancy Silverman

If you're interested in more of my books, be sure to follow my author page on Amazon (can be found on the link Bellow) or scan the QR-Code.

https://www.amazon.com/author/nancy-silverman

Printed in Great Britain
by Amazon